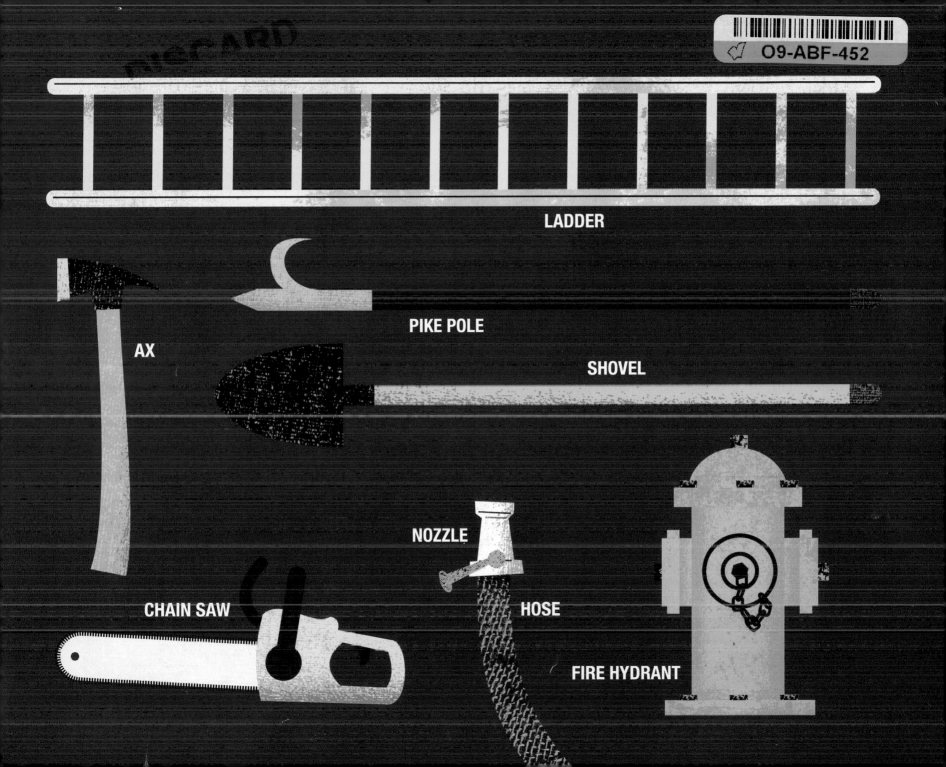

LADDER

PIKE POLE

AX

SHOVEL

NOZZLE

CHAIN SAW

HOSE

FIRE HYDRANT

O9-ABF-452

For Tien and Reid

Visit us on the Web! randomhousekids.com

Educators and librarians, for a variety of teaching tools, visit us at RHTeachersLibrarians.com

Library of Congress Cataloging-in-Publication Data
Austin, Mike, author, illustrator.
Fire engine no. 9 / by Mike Austin. — First edition.
 pages cm.
Summary: Follows a fire engine and its crew through a very busy day, using mainly sound words.
ISBN 978-0-553-51095-9 (trade) — ISBN 978-0-375-97428-1 (lib. bdg.) — ISBN 978-0-553-51096-6 (ebook)
[1. Fire engines—Fiction. 2. Fire fighters—Fiction.] I. Title. II. Title: Fire engine number nine. PZ7.A9253Fir 2015   [E]—dc23 2014016610

MANUFACTURED IN CHINA   10 9 8 7 6 5 4 3 2 1   First Edition

FIRE ENGINE No. 9

by Mike Austin

ENGINE NO. 9

Random House 🏠 New York

ALERT! ALERT!

FIRE!

FIRE!

FIRE!

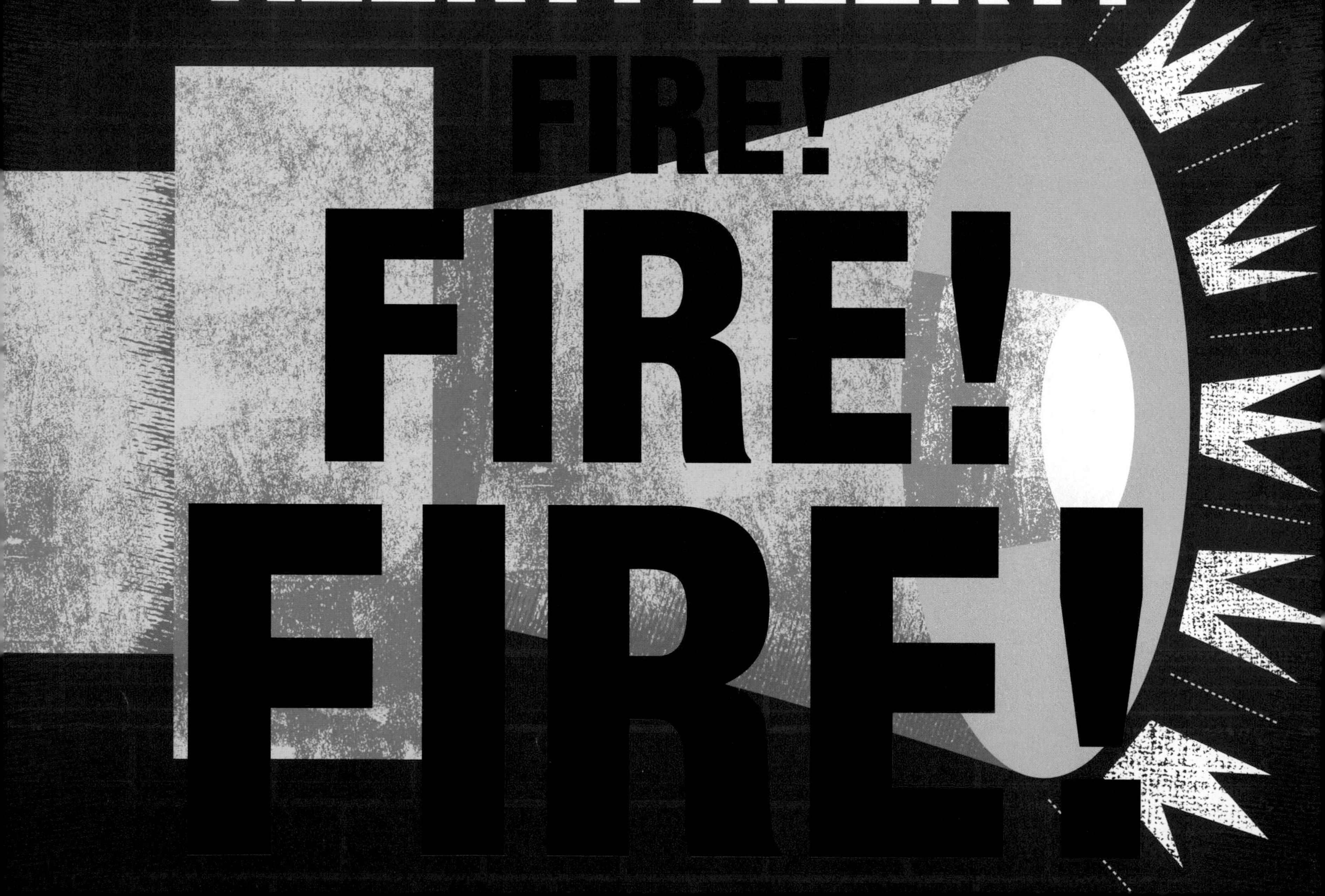

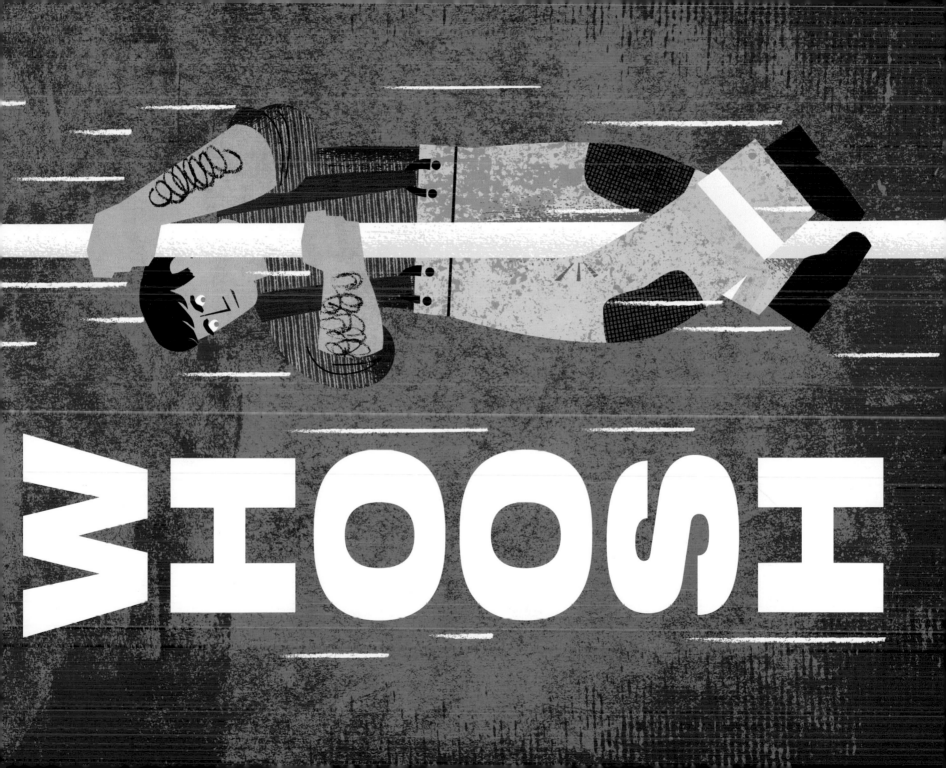

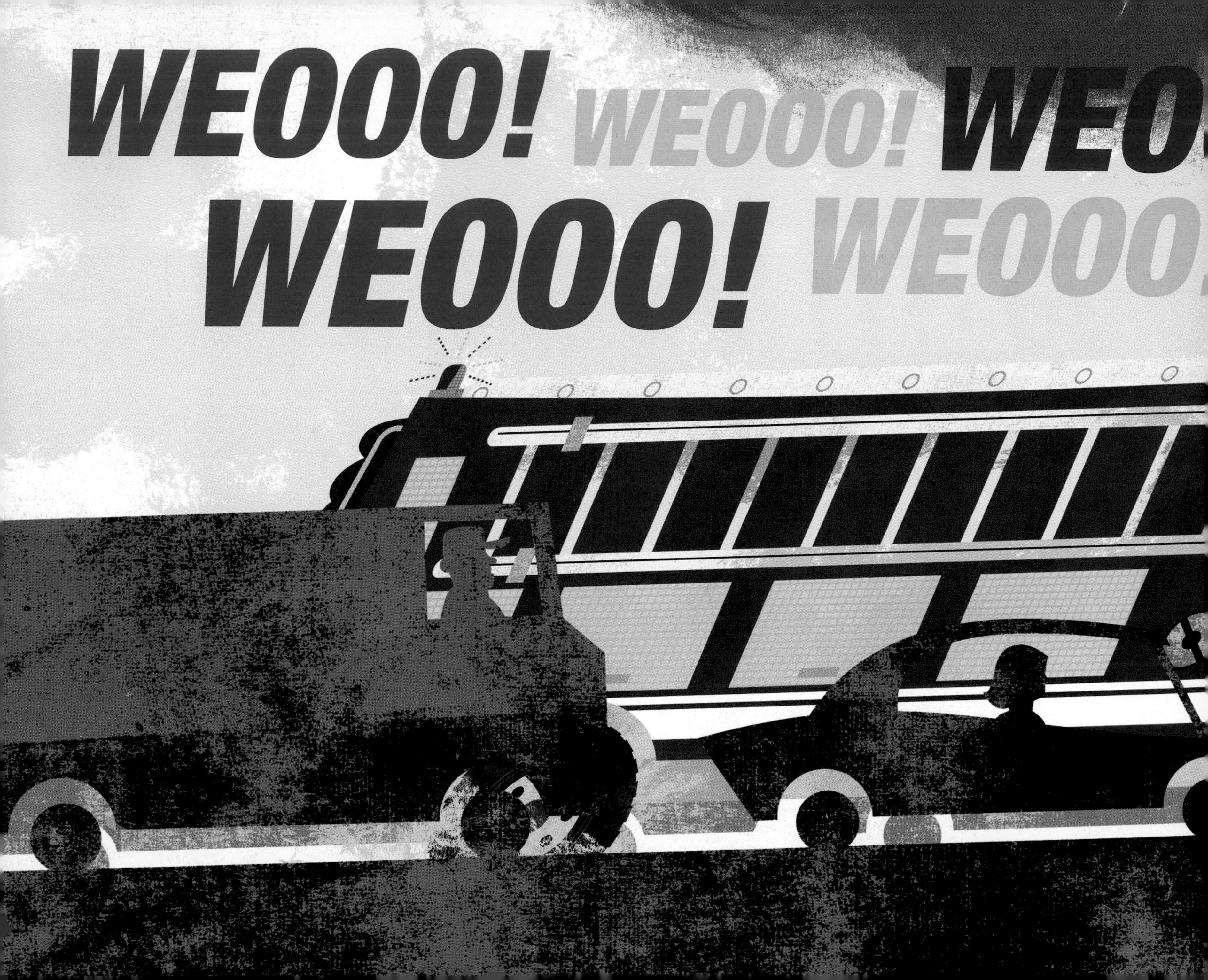
WEOOO! WEOOO! WEO
WEOOO! WEOOO

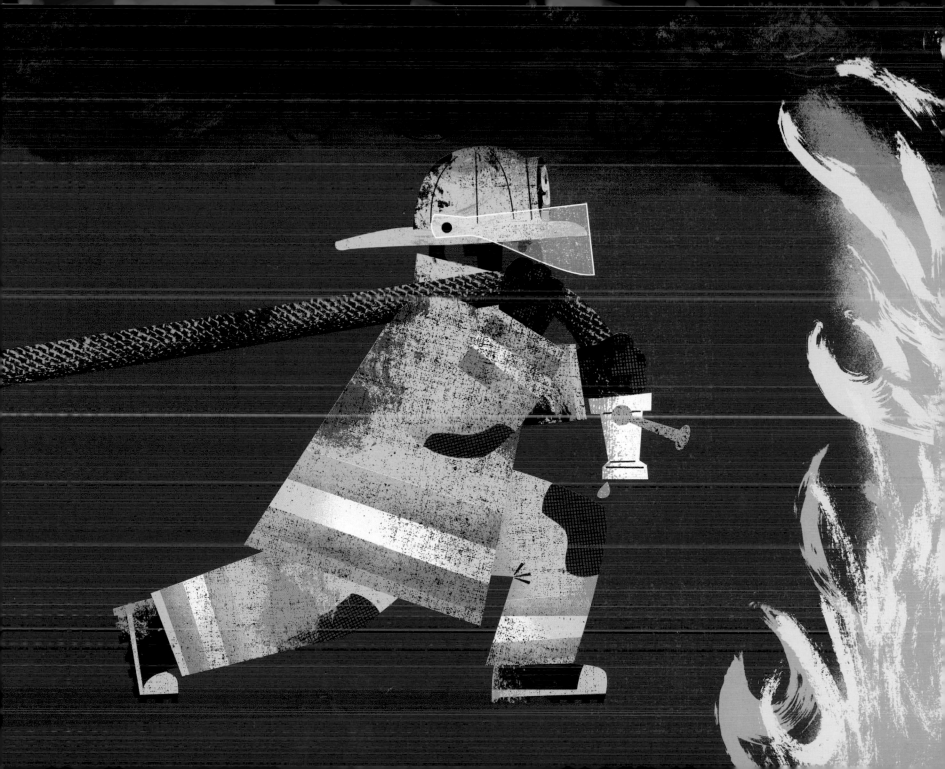

CLIMB! CLIMB! CLIMB!

CRAWL! CRAWL!

BEEP! BEEP! BEEP! BEEP! BEEP! BEEP!

What to Do During a Home Fire*

- Get low and go! Crawl under smoke to an exit. Heavy smoke and deadly gases collect along the ceiling.

- If you hear a smoke alarm, get out fast! You may only have a few seconds to escape.

- If smoke is blocking the door, use your second way out of the room or house.

- Feel the doorknob and door before opening it. If either is hot, leave the door closed and use the second way out.

- If you see smoke coming around the door, use the second way out.

- If you do open a door, open it slowly and be ready to shut it quick if there's smoke.

- Don't hide from firefighters! They may look scary with all of their equipment, but they are there to help you.

- Tell firefighters if there are any pets trapped in the house. Don't try to get them yourself!

- If your clothes catch on fire, stop, drop, and roll! Stop, drop to the ground, and cover your face with your hands. Then roll over and over or back and forth until the fire is out.

*Text is from "Be a Hero!" Federal Emergency Management Agency (FEMA), ready.gov/kids/know-the-facts/home-fires.

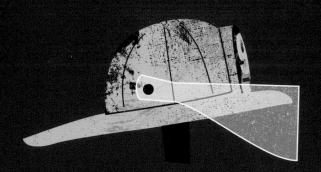

HELMET

SMOKE ALARM

FIRST-AID KIT

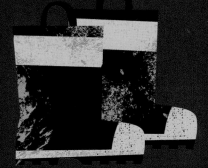

BOOTS

FIRE EXTINGUISHER

WALKIE-TALKIE

BULLHORN

FLASHLIGHT

GLOVES